For my daughter, Rebekah, who inspires her students every day —D.H.

For all the wonderful teachers at PS 321 —N.C.

Text copyright © 2017 by Deborah Hopkinson
Jacket art and interior illustrations copyright © 2017 by Nancy Carpenter
All rights reserved. Published in the United States by Schwartz & Wade Books,
an imprint of Random House Children's Books, a division of Penguin Random House LLC, New York.
Schwartz & Wade Books and the colophon are trademarks of Penguin Random House LLC.
Visit us on the Web! randomhousekids.com
Educators and librarians, for a variety of teaching tools, visit us at RHTeachersLibrarians.com
Library of Congress Cataloging-in-Publication Data
Hopkinson, Deborah.
A letter to my teacher / Deborah Hopkinson ; illustrated by Nancy Carpenter. — First edition.
pages cm
Summary: A letter from someone who was once an exasperating second grader reveals her experiences with a teacher who brought out the best in her.
ISBN 978-0-375-86845-0 (hc) — ISBN 978-0-375-96845-7 (glb) — ISBN 978-0-375-98776-2 (ebook)
[1. Teachers—Fiction. 2. Schools—Fiction. 3. Behavior—Fiction. 4. Letters—Fiction.] I. Carpenter, Nancy, illustrator. II. Title.
PZ7.H778125Let 2015
[E]—dc23
2013018299
The text of this book is set in Filosofia.
The illustrations were rendered in pen and ink and digital media.
MANUFACTURED IN CHINA
10 9 8 7 6 5 4 3
First Edition

a Letter to my Teacher

words by **Deborah Hopkinson**

pictures by **Nancy Carpenter**

schwartz & wade books • new york

Dear Teacher,

Whenever I had something to tell you,
I tugged on your shirt and whispered in your ear.
This time I'm writing a letter.

Dear Teacher,
Whenever I had somet
to tell you, I tugged on
and whispered in your
ear. This time I'm wr

I hope you remember me.

I was the one who marched to school that first day,

splashing through every puddle I could find.

I wore a bright yellow raincoat and a dark, stormy frown—

because for me, school meant sitting still and listening,

two things I wasn't much good at.

I stood there ornery and dripping,

just sure I'd get in trouble.

But instead you grinned at me.

"Good morning! Look at you,

standing there like Mary Kingsley

just back from canoeing up the Ogooué River."

"Who?" I said. "Where?"

"Mary Kingsley, the fearless explorer," you explained.

"Someday we'll read about her—and crocodiles.

Now get the mop."

Crocodiles!

After taking attendance, you made a big announcement:
"Welcome! This year we'll be planting the first-ever
Second-Grade Garden.
It will be our great experiment."
"Yay! We get to dig in the mud!" I shouted.

"True, but first we read about plants," you said.
"We'll use math to measure our plot,
and we'll write our garden plan."
Reading? Math? Writing?
I was better at running and jumping.

The next week we visited the creek behind the school to learn about plants and water.

When you weren't watching, I started to hop the rocks.

Right in the middle I got stuck.

"Look at me! I'm Mary What's-Her-Name," I hollered,

trying to sound brave.

"Watch out for crocodiles," you called back.

Then you rushed to rescue me.

On the way back, you held my hand,
and never told anyone how much I was shaking.

All fall, I tried hard to sit still.

Right before Thanksgiving vacation,

you asked who wanted to take the Mouse Brothers home.

"Me! Pick me!" I shouted.

But while I was busy eating turkey, my cat, Lucy, ate one brother.

I bought a replacement mouse. Except I just couldn't tell you.

One day when we were cleaning their cage,
you called me over to your desk and told me that
we might have to change the brothers' names
to Ma and Pa Mouse.
"You knew the whole time," I said.
Laughing, you said, "Might as well get used to it:
teachers see everything."

When winter came,

the reading corner became our secret garden of stories.

On Friday afternoons, we all curled up in a heap to listen—

just like our new litter of mice.

I loved it when you read to us, and always begged for more.

But I hated being called on to read out loud.

I kept tripping over words.

Once, right before my turn, I yelled,
"Raise your hand if you want to go home!"

Another time I clutched my throat and croaked,
"Uh-oh! I lost my voice."

Nothing fooled you, though.

You called me to your desk and asked,

"When we make our garden,

do you think the seeds will grow right away?"

"No!" I said. "Everyone knows they need time and sun and water."

"Well, learning to read takes time, too," you said.

"Now, I think you have a cat."

I nodded. "Lucy, the one who likes mice."

"I'd like you to read to Lucy every day," you suggested.

"It might keep her out of trouble."

I giggled. "Maybe I'll read her *Puss in Boots*!"

I practiced hard and you gave me extra help, too.

One day you brought me a special book.

"I met a real author and he autographed it

just for you," you said.

I looked at the cover and sounded out the words.

"Wow! It's about her! That explorer, Mary Kingsley."

You smiled. "Next week, you can share it with the class."

In March we explored our town.

We went on a field trip to an old house.

It was full of history—and secret stairways.

When I slipped away to look for
hidden treasure in the root cellar,
you and the whole class had to trudge down
the old stone steps to find me.
I think even you lost your patience that time.
"Exasperating" was the word you used.
I remember because that night
my mom helped me look it up in the dictionary.

The day you brought in seeds for us to choose,
I tugged on your shirt. "Can we plant this kind?
The packet says 'early spring.'
We can have bright red radishes in just a few weeks."
"Good reading and great idea!" you said.

Thanks to the math games we played,
measuring our garden patch was easy.
At last we turned over our soil and were ready to plant.
I was Radish Crew Chief
and read out the instructions all by myself.

All spring we weeded and watered
and kept garden journals, too.

On the Friday before summer vacation,
we wrote out invitations to every class
to come enjoy the salad we'd grown ourselves.
"Splendid spinach," said the principal.
"It's because of the worms," I explained.

I didn't know how to say thank you.
So on the last day I gave you a present:
a memory quilt.

I'd measured squares on paper and made
the story of our year in each one:
the reading corner,
worms in our compost,
the Magnificent Mouse Family,
and, best of all, a picture of you and me.
You looked at the quilt a long time,
then held it up for everyone to see.
"Thank you. Now I'll never forget you all,
and the Year of the Second-Grade Garden."
"Me neither," I promised.
And I never have.

For a long time now
I've been wanting to write to tell you
that even though I didn't always listen,
and I know I was exasperating,
second grade really was the best year ever.

So I guess you won't be too surprised to hear
that I still like to stomp through creeks,
dig in the garden,
and even read out loud to my cat.

Most of all I want to tell you
that I'm about to start my first job.
And tomorrow morning, when I go to work,
I'll think about everything you helped me explore,
and try my best to be like you.

Thank you for being my teacher.

—Your student